YOUR ISM
MY TISM

"Nothing in this world is impossible except for everybody doing the impossible"

-Aditya Mehla

Author'S Note

I mean to become an author like I did is just so incredibly amazing; I mean at one point in my life I was like okay adi boy accept the fact that you will never be great at something you have to use your brain to be great at and my god made me an author and not just an author; he made me the greatest writer of all times which is just beyond anything I could have ever imagined or wished for. I mean if like five ten years back you had found me and sat me down and told me the greatest writer would be from your country; I would have been like wow, really that's unbelievable; if you had been like from your state I would have lost it; I would have probably said you sir can eat anything you want; I would take care of it and if you had said from your own city I would have said you sir you gather your family and friends and you throw a massive party and its on me; this is such a great matter but for me to myself becoming the greatest writer of all times is just like unbelievable. I mean we can climb the scale this way also with how I would have accepted just being a writer to a okay okay writer but to be the greatest writer of all times, I mean wow. You guys should have seen me in literature class like I did not understand a word like for me the teacher was saying some kind of spells or something you know what I mean like I have this friend who likes eats things expired like all the time and he would somehow raise his arm and answer it correctly whenever our teacher would ask question but me oh boy they were like can you like think at all, boy like does it hurt when you think and I was like it does yes a little and look at me today here I sit as the greatest writer of all time. I can only imagine how crazy that dude who is considered the greatest who used to write plays and poems and stuff; I forgot his name but anyways he must be going up there like come on God you are making this idiot the greatest writer of all times? God would be like yeah, I am feeling that anything is possible vibe now a days plus so many people are like starting to doubt if God has a sense of humour or not and so I have to prove them wrong too and the dude must be like please God not this fool; put my soul in some body and put me back in the action; I can't see this everyday and God be like you calm down and sit down okay.

Has there ever been a better start to a book than this? I wouldn't think so but then again when have I ever read a book like in my dreams or something as people like to say but nonetheless I think it's a great start. This is my 10th book so that's special too. In all seriousness though I wanted to be a writer so I talked to some people who write; I mean they are not like big writer's but still there attitude was basically that we choose writing because this is the only occupation when you can do anything like you have to search for ideas and so take a vacation and see new things and gather information or something but for me I wanted to write because I had ideas; I didn't decide to be a writer and then think of idea's; I mean now that I am here writing 10th book; now I am looking for ideas but I didn't get into it with that and plus I believe you get ideas either way when you are happy or sad you know what I mean; when you are sad we tend to think about the things causing the sadness but due to this habit of writing I can like channel it somewhere else which I am extremely grateful for and also I have utmost faith in God and I believe he will take care off things that are out of my control. So, anyways hopefully you have a good read.

Ohh wait actually I do need to tell you how I got into writing. I mean i have this story and like I was waiting for somebody to ask me so how did you got into writing or why you got into writing but nobody I know has come close to asking that question so I have to get it off my chest somewhere and this is perfect timing I believe so here It goes so I was in my class 4th right and we had this ▯nglish literature teacher and she was the strictest teacher of all times like she was always in bad mood for some reason like everyday for 8 of those school hours and I personally believe it is very hard to always be hard on kids like all the time you know what I mean but anyways this one day she was like I have to check some copies and so every one of you guys write three paragraphs on how you guys celebrated your birthday while I correct these notebooks or whatever and the funniest kid in our class said but I have not celebrated my birthday yet; it's in two months and I laughed and now that I think about it; It was the least funny thing ever and he was not funny at all really; I was just pretty darn dumb at that time in like figuring out what's funny and what's not like for most kids parents like hiding behind some toy and then appearing and going hoo like stays funny till they are like 1 or something but for me like I believe like my parents have stopped doing it but if they had carried on with it I would probably have giggled to it even today so you know. Anyways, I didn't write because I was at the last seat and there was very little time for her to go to everyone before the bell rings even if she starts with my row; she at best can do like 6 kid's maybe 7 but in my row there were 12 kids so I was cool but then all of a sudden as our class was being loud; she stood up and said okay and randomly picked a kid and asked him to come in the front and say it and I was like oh no she is picking randomly; she will definitely pick one of us like between me and me friend because we were sitting on the last bench and when it comes to randomly the last benchers are always in trouble you know what I mean so I started writing like quickly and she did pick me; I went number four and asked me to come in front of the class and read it to everyone loudly and I remember being very nervous like almost shaking because as I said she was the strictest teacher of all times and so I don't remember what I wrote but by 4th or 5 line she started smiling and she smiled all through it and at the end of it she was like that's how you do it; he picks things so beautifully; that was amazing, kid; go back to your seat and everyone clap for him and I have never had this amazing feeling before but that was amazing. Anyways, years pass and all the articles and essay I wrote after that in school like I always got C or D or whatever like some of them were appreciated but in like a very negative way. Anyways, so I finish my college and then I am like i am in my 20s now; I have to like find something to do which like I like doing you know as they say in all the motivational videos you know because my parents take all my big decisions you know because I don't want to take chances but after college I have to find something like what's my purpose and people actually also started asking like what's your plan and I would tell them like whatever and they be like okay that's great but what is it that you like doing and you want to be you know what I mean and I was tired of all these chasing dream thing and so I was asking myself seriously like there has to be something you know what I mean and one day I went to bed and I closed my eyes waiting to fall asleep and suddenly that 4th class day popped in out of nowhere and that's when I was like okay this is what I am going to be and dedicate myself to and I started like reading all these books and not just books but the best seller's books and I was like they obviously read a lot and the stuff like they don't like in their book; they write it in own book in their own way with like correct way that they thing in their mind you know what I mean like imagine an argument between two people but instead of arguing face to face they are writing in in their books you know what I mean and I am not saying they are not great or they are not better writers than me; that's not what I am saying at all but I am like I should stop reading everything literally you know what I mean like I am going to do it my way because If you read something and you have a thinking brain after some time you will be like okay wait I can say it better and I don't like it this way like in science like this scientist did this experiment in 1890 and then this scientist made it better in 1913 you know what I mean like maybe my approach is wrong maybe it's right I don't know you be the judge and time will tell I guess.

Chapter-1
Sadness

Sadness is underqualified; it has no right to be around you but it gets you on the basis of pure confidence you know what I mean. Sadness is like a very very good sales dude that you figure out years later that every word he said was nothing but a lie you know what I mean and that is if you figure that out. You know those sales guy like you find something iffy about them and you go to them with like a million things in your head and you are like I don't even care where my anger leads to; he's been feeding me lies for the past so many years; I am going to scream at him so loud and you get there but these salesman reverse it like you was supposed to find out about this and this was all for the good and it doesn't changes anything you know what I mean or like other side is even more lier and you come home feeling all stupid and everything even though you know you are right and he's playing me again but still you feel like there's nothing to do; then you start to get more things to say to him when you are home but whenever you face that guy; you are dead silent. He has total control over you for some reason; he's that good. We have to be like our elder's I guess. You ever go in a shop and there's like a old guy who keeps screaming even though salesman is making sense like get me this and salesman is like sir it's out of my control; you have to talk to the company but the old guy keeps screaming I don't give a care and you are standing there like why is he screaming so loud on this innocent salesman; he should calm down but that's exactly what we need to do; Don't listen to what sadness says; just scream. When it makes sense scream louder. We are all in this weird habit from the movies where they like make sadness look cool you know what I mean like this guy is living with so much pain; he has this amazing will power or whatever and still he goes on but the thing about the movie is they never show what the bad guy is going through; he's not happy either; he's in deep pain too you know what I mean and even the good guy like he can't sleep at night because of bad dreams and it looks cool like he doesn't sleep at all but he doesn't yawn at all either during the day you know what I mean like stop chasing that; you are setting yourself up to be like that like I should have pain in my heart too for me to be like that and it's not cool. It will not look cool; you will seriously be sad and in pain; look for happiness. Don't watch a lot of movie's; every good guy is going to be sad. Listen to what actors who played those sad roles say after it especially the actors who go deep with their roles; some of them take so much time to recover and then you see their photos in the newspaper and you are like what happened to him? Sadness happened to him; that's what happened. That's real sadness; that's what really happens when you move around with a lot of pain in your heart. When you start to look at the world like that you know what I mean.

Also, your work is your first wife; you can't run away from it so if your work is making you not happy then just pack it up and leave. Sometimes we find a person with whom you can go through anything like and it's fine because you start to do for them and you start to suffer for them which doesn't bother you at all and that's perfectly fine; when you decide to live for others obviously it gets easier but sometimes we don't find true love like that no matter how hard we try; couples who live together all their lives are still not it sometimes you know what I mean so find something that makes you happy and reverse the whole situation like no matter what's happening in my personal life; when I am at work I am happy because even if you do find that true love; there will still be ups and down in your personal life; maybe your partner would go through something which you can't help them with at all you know what I mean so finding something that you love doing as a professional should be the top most priority. Now when people hear that, they think of money and fame like the jobs that have them are the happy job's which is not the case. So many people don't know what they want to do but they want money and fame. Even if they fall in love with the job that brings money and fame; once you get the money and the fame; what do you do now? Always always aim to be best; the greatest at something. Whatever it maybe like nobody anywhere in any country should be better at it than you or at least you should be in the conversation for the best because then you are going to have to keep going all the time and also you can't be the best if you don't love it and like it genuinely. Plus, what's the thing that brings us the most happiness; we talking and people in awe of what we are saying. Now even if you are very rich; people will talk; you will not have the stage all the time; like everybody would not be impressed with you; some people you probably won't even feel superior like I have this car that turns into an helicopter; oh just helicopter mine turns into a helicopter and a road you know what I mean like you won't ever win but when you are the greatest at it; they won't relate to you; the stage is always yours even if you are sitting in the room with people at your level; all of you have different stories of how you got there and how you think and how your brain works and all those things like you will always feel great being great you know what I mean.

We learn from love stories of two people you know but there's far greater learnings in the love story of an individual like how they didn't at the start but they rediscovered it you know because to move onto the two people love stories you have to believe you are the best possible person for them; that them looking for somebody else would be a foolish mistake; without the love for yourself; there would just be a lot of doubt, no trust and fights and sometimes when there is a lot of that even if you love the person you feel like leaving them would be the best possible decision for the both of you so watch more and read more of the individual love stories and it's harder to make yourself love yourself rather than making somebody else love you because you know the exact truth about them; you don't judge yourself but that's the thing about brain; it can make you think it's gone but deep down when the crucial times comes those things will show up like it owns the biggest house in your brain so maybe the people leaving inside it aren't social at all and keep to themselves all the time but when the house is on fire they will come out no matter what you know what I mean. Like that can't past so to accept your flaws and to understand that you can't learn without mistakes; you can't be perfect; sometimes you don't even realise till later that you were so wrong; all of it comes from mistakes. We are actually lucky to realise all this because people who don't; well you would have to be worse than them to like them you know what I mean. Like when I was young I was making joke over something over and over again and my mom was like why can't you let things go and I had this moment of realisation like yeah actually I am like that; I have had instances where I have made things awkward by keep going on and on and I always wanted to change that about myself but I wasn't really able to and now as I have grown up I have realised that It is one of my biggest strength; to be going on and on about something; if it wasn't for that I probably won't be writing this book today.

Also, there should be a bigger word than love for love and sacrifice combined thing probably lovice or something because every single person on this planet is in love but a very small amount of that will sacrifice; it's so rare that there's actually isn't even a word for that; there's true love but that's still love. Love is figuring out what's best for the person you love not for yourself and if it comes to that that it's not you who she will be happiest with even though there shouldn't be because if you love them; you will do anything for their happiness but still if it comes to that they will be more happy elsewhere; then you being willing to let them go; accepting the fact that you probably won't see them ever again; love and sacrifice is so rare; almost not there. To be clear mother's love is love and sacrifice; I am not talking about that; you know what I talking about, right? Well, I sure hope you do. A mother or a father would do it if it comes to that but other than that people need to have the people around them and when they don't even if that person is happy; it makes them not happy which basically means you are putting yourself above them which is still love like don't get me wrong but love and sacrifice is far bigger than love and we need a word for that. You are actually hoping that they are not happy and being with you would change that which reminds me sadness can sometimes often come from dreaming for other people's failure you know what I mean and if that is the reason for your sadness then you need to remember that there has never been a person in the history as you and there won't ever be; God has set us up with strength and things that are not our strengths but both of them are basically our strength if you can break them down and understand them; don't try to change them like focusing on not doing the things that you aren't great at; focus on doing more of things you are great at; keep working on things you are great at; that is the best way to hide things you aren't great at because people focus too much on things that aren't their strength and making them their strength that they leave the things that are their strength unworked on you know what I mean and when you start working on things you are great at; you won't feel the need to dream for their failures; you would start feeling even with everything they have got; they don't have you and rightly so. Prove God right; he has given you all the characteristics you have for a reason; everything doesn't happen for a reason; you have your characteristics for anything and everything and they pop up in whatever situation; you never had to use them in the past so you think ohh that's new but no you are born with everything and there's a reason for all your flaws too; if you had not flaws or backside then you will have to love every single body; it will hurt you to not be with the person no matter how imperfect they are for you then to be happy that you are with the person that gets you; actually you would be all alone because nobody would be able to relate to you so you will be worried and sad all the time; imperfections and our flaws are the things that makes us or gets us happy then the other thing you know what I mean. It's a major huge thing to remember; your imperfections get you happiness not your perfections. If I was giving a speech or if this was an audiobook; I would repeat it like 10-12 times; I want you guys to know that. I am talking about God given imperfections not the ones you pick up along the way; those are toxic; they are like sometimes you know you hear somebody say a catchphrase and you are like that's not good but other people like it so later on somewhere else you find yourself using it you know what I mean; those traits are like that; they get in even if you don't want to sometimes and they cause sadness not the one's we were born with. Your perfections pleases other people not yourself like let's say you help somebody with something; that's great but them saying thank you and you feeling good from that thank you; that's imperfection right expecting something for your good deed, right? But that's what gets us happiness so try to not pick up anything along the way; just be yourself; we are great!

Be the person people fall in love with; some people are born with it you know what I mean like I am great; everybody loves me but if they are not born with that; they never figure it out;

things can change; if you don't feel like I am not a person people can fall in love with; instead of just sleeping on it day after day ask yourself why? Most likely you won't get an answer; then stop believing that or ask people around you to be honest with you and say what they would change about you; ask those people only who has been there for many years and if you do gets answers on your own just work on whatever it is and improve that. First and foremost you can fall in love without any reasons; that's the great bit but still give them reasons to; ask them sometimes why do you love me? Because if there's a reason then there's good chance you will stay in love forever.

When you think things will get better it gets worse and then when you think okay this is permanent like I am here forever things get better but happiness is not vice versa you know when you make up your mind to be happy or trying to find some kind of happiness in every situation you would be happy or at the very least not bothered. Bad things don't stop happening in nobody life so let your brain get happy from things happening to them and your heart from you helping everybody you know what I mean. Sometimes our happiness comes from other people's failing and thats okay you can't help it; when good things are happening for other people and not so good to you then it's natural I guess to feel like that but you can't be the reason somebody's failing; your brain plays tricks on you; it always shows our situation in a bad light and other's as not a big deal light when they are in some kind of trouble so be happy I guess if they are failing but do everything in your power to help them; that way there would be no kind of conflict in your heart; I helped and gave my all to his but he still failed because if you don't help and they fail then if you are a good person it will tell you; you are a bad person; a good person's brain is just the dude who doesn't want to agree and has to move in other direction in all the arguments you know what I mean. what I am saying. Another thing is most people are always thinking on the lines of missing like if I don't go online or stay off or something would they miss me or if I don't go to this party would they miss me and their happiness depends on that for some reason and they should miss you but the sad part is you can be the very best and still you won't be missed you know like I am a huge basketball ball and I am a huge Steph curry and Klay Thompson fan and so i only used to watch the golden state warriors(the team They both play for) games till last year for or if like some other important playoff game is in clutch time and it's very close or something but my point is this year they both were injured and out for the whole year but I am watching basketball and now I am deeper in basketball now you know what I mean so my point being you only think about being missed in the moment like wow I will miss this or that but we are programmed in such a way that our minds can get used to everything; like it will stop missing anything after some time; I mean obviously it's hard when the person you love leave and you miss them but you will only miss them till you don't allow people to walk in; as soon as you allow them to walk in you won't miss the person you loved as much. It is a matter of fact that you can be the absolute best and you won't be missed even LeBron James who's the best basketball player; from where I am from people know only one current player and that's him and he missed the play-offs last season but he wasn't missed at least the game didn't; I am sure some of his fans did but I am sure they got used to it too but most importantly the game didn't miss him like the playoffs were fantastic you know what I mean and that's my point you can't sit around and wonder if you are going to be missed because yeah you will be for a few time but eventually you will not be missed; some people won't be forgotten but they are not missed you know if your work is so great then you can't be forgotten obviously; heck if your work is super; your work will be made familiar to the new generation but nobody will miss you; after some time they won't stop partying because you are not there you know. People are like movies like you are like I will never watch something better; this is the greatest movie of all time but well you watch the next movie and it's fantastic because everything's different so nobody even knows how good that would feel. They are those movie that you will find epic and will take a close place in your heart but that doesn't mean you are gonna watch that movie ever again in your life you know what I mean.

Chapter-2
Failing

There is a huge difference between working hard and working till you can't you know like a person working whole day and then turning his laptop off brushing his teeth; going to bed tired and between a person falling asleep working. There is a huge huge difference but you know you can be as motivated as you possibly can be still not be able to fall asleep doing what you want to do that you think is important heck a necessity for your life; you just can't do that till you have failed many times; it can't be taught; it can't be learned; it just comes when you fail again and again and everybody you know is laughing at you you know what I mean. Failing is a blessing for so much more; when you fail at something and still make it your priority you can do so much more than you can with success even if they are the humblest person ever; you know as they say you have to be arrogant when you are not there and humblest if that's a word when you there but you know usually it's reverse you know. Patience is the other thing that comes with failure and I believe being patient is the only thing a man can do perfectly in his lifetime; all the other things in life you can be the best at and still not be able to do it perfectly like there will always be scope for improvement but patience is the only thing that can be done perfectly. there is not an inch of scope of improvement; you just stay with it till you acheive it and it's done perfectly. You stay exactly the same in failure you know because people they keep believing but they mature; they start taking their work seriously; there is no joy left in it you know; they stop doing or thinking their initial thought when they started what they started off with was being unique you know; they start analyzing other people and what they did and how to do it and so they start walking on those lines; trying to copy other's; they think they are doing their own work but you can see shadows off other people's work in their work. Don't get me wrong they can still acheive success and what have you but it won't be the same even they themselves won't take pride in their work so you know it's like food if it goes in another pipe no matter if you are eating sweet sweet ice cream it will taste sour; it will only taste so good if it stays down the path that it was going and plus you learn a whole lot more and experience a whole lot more when you are being you; youknow what I mean. It will be like you know sometimes you don't know anything about this house you are trying to find; you have never been in that neighborhood so you will ask around and find that house in quicker time than second time around when you know there's a big tree close to the house and there's this sign there because now you are looking for big tree and sign instead of the house you know what I mean. Most people can go on and on for days when you ask them tell us something about themselves but they can't put a sentence together if you ask them why are their different; what makes you stand out? They can't start the sentence; they will go well I think; well; I think then a loud I think and then they will stop for a second and make something up which will sound stupid because there is no answer to that question why are you different than everybody else? You can't put who you think or how you work in word's; nothing you answer will sound like okay yeah nobody else ever is like that you know what I mean; it's just your confidence that can tell okay yeah he's a different animal you know; how you take this question is the answer to this question.

Plus, I think sometimes you can work so hard and there's nothing and you stop doing it and people miss that and they realise okay he might walk away and they start appreciating you differently now and you realise how good you are you know by taking a break and not doing anything; sometimes you have to not do anything just sit on your ass for some time for things to get better; both positive and negative approach will make it worse. Like trick questions there are trick situation's in life where you have to do nothing; just walk away or keep walking you know what I mean. So, all in all main point is you get into something because you believe you can do something that nobody else can; you have something that nobody else has and after a few failures you sit on that no I am not special; I don't have nothing new to offer to this field but you still stay in that field you know; either leave the field or keep believing; don't give up and still keep going you know what I mean. Not every field has the luxury of education you know that you learn somebody else's work and become a teacher and give that to young people; you don't have that; you are either the one making the information or you are not needed in other fields you know what I mean.

There is no need to listen to people either; I mean you should hear to intelligent people but who really can tell who is an intelligent person? Most people make wrong turn all their lives but they have such a beautiful explanation for everything that you think ohh okay they are intelligent but they are not. Let's say it's a sunny hot summer day and you have just enough funds for either ice cream or something spicy and you want to have an ice cream but your friends gives you 20 reasons for burgers and you go for burgers; you would think that's a good decision because well your friend gave such a beautiful explanation where everything's covered and it sounds like a logical choice especially since your lips never touched the ice cream but in reality it was not; it was for him because he

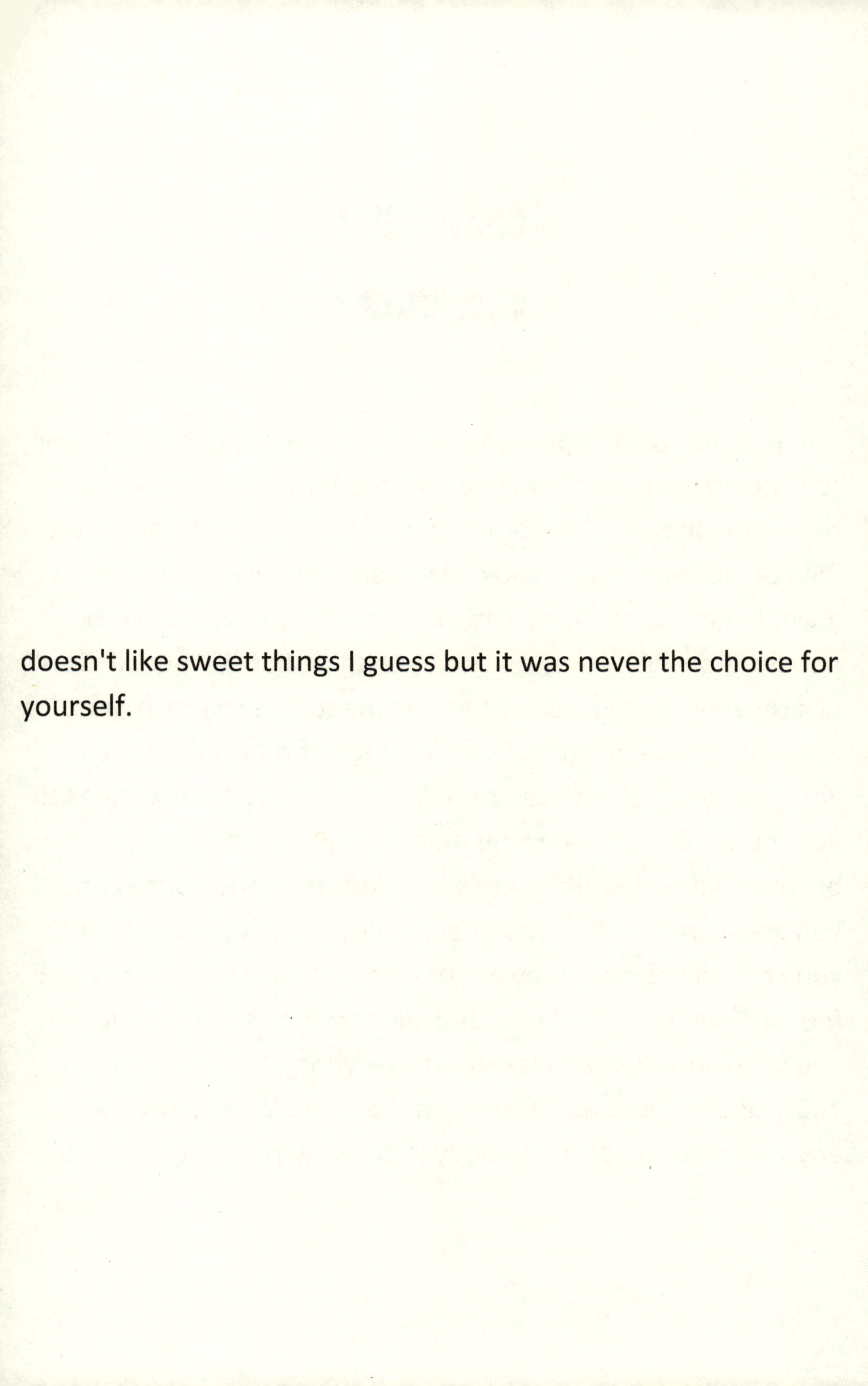

doesn't like sweet things I guess but it was never the choice for yourself.

CHAPTER-3
Acceptance

I think that most people can only accept other people a step or two step from where they are you know what I mean like if they think they are 20% brave they can only accept people are 25% brave even if they know like there are people who are like a whole lot braver than them like army people you know like people know what they do and everything but still people Don't or probably can't like accept that somebody is so much more than them or they have this false image of themselves like I would do it; i just choose not to because I have better things to do. This is all when we know these things like you can tell how brave you are by like if there's a cockroach in the house and you are scared of it and somebody picks it up like nothing then you can tell like okay they are braver than me but the things of feelings like feelings of love and all that; they are impossible to know because first and foremost everybody think they are at 100% of them and there be no way of knowing anything else anyways or probably everybody is at 100% in love; there's no

50% or things like that. I don't know what this percentage is supposed to mean you know; I just took it to you know go on about that people are not willing to accept too far from themselves like somebody has some attribute that is 50-60 times themselves and they will never be able to have that ever In their life's because you see all these movie's and people come back home and start imagining themselves doing that and feel great actually but in reality they will never do it even the movie guy didn't do it; I mean they did did it but with all kinds of necessary protection and all that I am sure you know what I mean; nobody comes home and be like that was amazing and I would never be able to do that and that's great because if movie's start bringing reality and eye opening about themselves then what are we supposed to watch to make us feel good when we don't. The people who accept that there are people and all that like so much better at conversation and making friends they fall into sadness; it's is pretty hard to fully accept what you are and be happy. Especially when you compare yourself to somebody many percentage better than you; I mean that lasts forever but when you compare to people who are less braver and everything it does cheer you up but it lasts for only some time. People try so hard to make somebody less than them in things that can't be seen you know like bravery like ohh you didn't come to college because you were sick; if I was sick I would run a marathon. Best people think afterwards not before and go into a situation with whatever happens happens mentality you know like afterwards they be like what if this had happened? Oh can you imagine? That would have been horrible. They go to bed feeling all cringy you know what I mean but most of us; we think beforehand what if this and this happens and we go to bed all comfortable thinking we avoided it and most of it is baseless like how would you know what is going to happen when you have never been in that situation. I mean some assumptions are good like you should think okay this is a long race and I will get tired; very tired so I will need to will it out and I am prepared for that but we here thinking I will definitely pull my groin and hamstring and I will fall on the ground in the middle of the race due to extreme dehydration and so I shouldn't participate in the race; what's the point of completing half race? It's the same as not completing except you made a fool out of yourself and why would I want that? That is why we are here at 10%; you don't go directly to 80% you know. When you get used to it and you get to like 20-30% you understand I can do it and what it will take and then this beautiful journey start that you don't dislike at all; you fall in love with that journey; I mean every now and then you will wish like wish I could get to 80% tomorrow or as fast as possible but you know you would be able to brush off that frustration quite easily I believe even if you don't when you have seen what it's required to get to those people's position you stop forcing yourself to find something bad in other people like yeah Cristiano is good but man he's arrogant you know like if we worked as hard as he does and eat what he eats we will probably be like wow if I work this hard everyday for years for so many years of my life; I probably tell everybody I am a better footballer than them. Heck, it be the only conversation I would ever be interested in having. Sir, how are you? I am the best footballer in the world; that's how I am. Okay sir; how would you like your suit; I would like my suit as the best footballer on the planet you know what I mean. Another lesson from football is most amateur footballers when they get a pass they will look at the whole ground to pass to except from the player he got the pass from you know what I mean who is the most open man on the ground; now when players become professional they have a better understanding of everything after being coached or whatever they rectify that but in life there are no coaches to most people; most people don't want to learn anything because everybody is right and we are going to keep thinking that due to internet now because it is set up to always make us feel right, right? But we have to accept and learn from as I said that open man football example that the people who are helping us might need our help too; we often neglect that man but we have to be there for him more than anybody I feel.

Chapter-4
Mistakes

I think there are lessons to be learned from mistakes not stupidity; the only lesson from stupidity is to not do that ever again you know what I mean. Most people they are doing stupid things thinking they are making mistakes and vice versa too like Sometimes things go so bad or so far away from plan; people start to think it was stupid but no you just committed a mistake. Mistakes is not in negative sense at all you know; mistakes is a very positive thing; it means you don't exactly know where your aunt live and so you decide to go and meet her one day and you take a left instead of a right or something and it takes you 5 hours instead of 2 hours to get to her house which you learn from like okay next time I am here I take the right turn I will save myself some hours. The way we are set up as humans; we are bound to make mistakes anyways you know; sometimes there are things on our chest and you are like no no it will pass with time but it doesn't so you feel like okay I will get it out in the open that will surely take this burden off my back you know but you say it now you feel more burdened that I shouldn't have said it; it's a stupid thing to do and you know if the other person reacts positively it's good if they don't it's a mistake which is not a mistake either ways; the next time you feel this way again you have to do it all again; you have to keep doing it again and again no matter what; there's nothing to learn from these kind of mistakes; it's bound to happen; till one day you found success with that and all the past mistakes Don't seem like mistake you know what I mean like there's nothing to learn from some mistakes but you suceed and they are not mistakes; they were just steps. It is like let's say you sit in an exam and you made couple of mistakes in some questions but you passed so there's no need to think about those mistakes if you are on the path of your goal or like learning how to drive a cycle you know; you can come home and be like I was not doing that right or whatever so I will watch a couple of videos on youtube or ask a few questions but there's no point; just go in and put in time; it will come naturally and all those falling down; now that wasn't a mistake, now was it? Now a days every thing is made of learning from your mistakes which you should do but not in everything sometimes it's just time especially when mistakes are being made on people; people meet somebody bad who is smooth and put their 100% trust in them and it turns out to be a mistake and what they learn from it is to not trust nobody you know which is stupid because not everybody's the same; everybody might think the same but all of us act differently you know what I mean; so now they are not going to put any trust in anybody which is only going to get them sadness because you can't work like that; you have to trust somebody which they will start to do in some time like it will take them some time but they will be right back from where they started you know what I mean so basically they just wasted time and I know it's not easy trusting somebody like that ever again and you might not be able to trust anybody like that ever again but you have to put some trust in somebody for it to be there and make us feel some kind of happiness and the sad part is though that most of the time we jump over people who we should have put our trust in to people we shouldn't have put our trust in you know what I mean; there are all kinds of people around everybody and that should be the lesson from that mistake I guess but not no trusting anybody and put the curtains on everything you know what I mean. I mean if you went into something too quick or didn't think too much or something that's a mistake but you analysed well and you still failed then it's not a mistake it's just something that happened;

now it's just about belief like would my style work or do I need to go back and change that. The thing to remember is when you come to the conclusion that okay my style won't work; I need to make some changes to my style; would the twerk in your style still keep you you or would you start to be a little like somebody else because then there's no point because you will never be able to do it as good as them anyways and you are not your original self either so you can't move or act naturally you know what I mean. Reacting to other people calling you out on mistakes that ain't even a mistake is also very difficult to mature; I mean this is my 10th book and all the people who know me and know that I write keep suggesting changes or whatever I should do but none of them have like even read it so how do they? You know what I mean; it's in our DNA to not keep our mouth shut on anything and you know the logical thing to do is not react and keep moving but sometimes they don't let us keep moving and it gets more harder to be silent you know and some people's philosophy is I don't want any differences with anybody but I am not going down in some stupid anybody's eyes either who won't help me in any situation which is I guess okay you know but I personally try to keep my mouth shut which i believe to be the hardest thing ever but you know you sleep a little late you know with all the things you could have said and it's annoying when the same sentence or dialogues keep popping back again and again but it is what it is I guess so overall what I was trying to say is mistakes are pretty darn cool if you ask me; who you make mistakes over is the real question and so if it's something that's worth it then it was not a mistake it was just something that happened you know like your car getting hit in a parking lot like it makes you feel angry but what could be done; it was just something that happened and if the mistake taught you something awesome than be glad for that mistake; mistakes make us clock things we have already heard or listened before you know what I mean.

Chapter-5

Good and the bad

This might be the stupidest thing ever that has come out of my mouth or I have written but the only people considered good are those who don't do anything you know what I mean like shouldn't it be like maybe they are bad maybe they are good but you go through all your life and not do anything and you are considered good, right? Only bad people have unity good people have so many differences and I don't know why like probably you need to be united to do bad stuff or it won't happen you know what I mean whereas you can do good stuff even alone. I don't know maybe good people don't clog it as well like if they hear something on tv or read it in newspapers like somebody kill somebody it doesn't move them at all and then they see some people smoking cigarettes or something outside their office or somewhere and they are on about culture of their place and how everything needs to change and how this is not a good environment to live for good people and good families. Maybe the thing is like when you do something bad you tell everybody with confidence but when you do something good you are supposed to keep it to yourself because people find you arrogant which it's not I feel you are just taking pride in yourself which is awesome you should take pride in yourself and should go on for as long because the only people who say it's arrogant are people who don't even help the people who have helped them in the past or is helping them in the present and they most certainly doubt if somebody promises to like help them in the future because their senses are telling them there's no help coming and it's only because if tables were turned you wouldn't have helped that person you know what I mean. For some reason it's okay to post as many food pics and Saturday night pics and all the good weather pics especially when they are not celebrities and most of their followers live in the exact same area and the funny thing about that Saturday night posts is the person they tag like to show this is the person who's with me enjoying to the fullest like comments right way in the comments section like what a crazy night and the super funny is when they make videos and like point the camera at the other person who is like just looking the other way not having fun at all it seems and as soon the camera's on them they just start jumping and screaming like yeah; shy people's yeah is amazing because they are worried how the stranger next to them is looking at them right so they can't like scream hard so they like just put their hand in hair like the statue of Liberty and they don't move no matter the video is 10 seconds long or 2 minutes long they are just standing there or they would start sipping anything or laughing like so anyways my whole point is you are supposed to show off like the way we are set up right now is to show off but you can't show off your goodness which shouldn't be the case like so many people post stuff like bought a new car and it's amazing and the engine is brand new or whatever but nobody ever posts like today I fed 2 pigeon's which is no big deal but makes me super happy about myself and I will keep helping someone everyday and keep Posting the same stuff everyday. People don't think before posting the ice cream recipes thinking they have cracked some kind of science code like you can basically add anything sweet to ice cream you know and it works; there's nothing great going on about what you just did but still the smile on their face and confidence in asking people to follow them for many more such recipes is so amazing and there's nothing bad with it; you keep doing stuff that makes you feel good about yourself till the day you die without thinking about what other people are thinking you know. It just doesn't make sense to me you know but I guess we have all sorts of people wired almost the same yet so different you know what I mean. Some people have like controlled half part of their brain's and half don't you know like if you tell them Jeff said you are an idiot; how do you respond; they would be like I don't care and they really don't care like it doesn't rile them up even by 0.01 percentage but you ask them to go and ask Jeff what time is it and they start worrying so much like they couldn't do it you know what I mean. The main point was that if good people come together and become United that's the only way for less bad in this world or this would go on but I guess bad people have that mindset because something has to happen for them to turn bad like there has to be a lot of pain and suffering I guess with no help whereas you are just good like nothing has to happen; you are just good you know what I mean but we should make good people stronger like the first thing they should be taught in school is it is absolutely compulsory to help like this whole year you help 500 people and you pass and if you don't you fail like stay in the open and help; not only would that keep less people from turning bad no matter what happens because now they know how amazing it feels to give back but also the love they will receive from the people they are helping will make them feel special you know what I mean and it will teach people how to help you know what I mean like if there's a bad motor bike accident and there's urgent needs off leader most people are like deer in the headlights you know what I mean like they are waiting for people to lead or give them instructions on what to do; some people just keep on moving and you would obviously still be treated and called good even when you don't help anybody as long as you are not the reason of or by people getting hurt you know what I mean and that's the damn problem so I guess school needs to teach how to be united in good and bring it in culture like automatically guy walks in the situation and sees 7 people doing something good and you automatically realise what you need to do and you start doing it you know what I mean. The other thing is coolness which is a huge factor in everything everybody knows that and all I got to say about that is it's easy to do cool things but it's super hard to do things that aren't cool and make them look cool you know what I mean. no actually that was stupid; it isn't easy to do cool things; it's pretty hard actually and very dangerous and that is what makes them look cool actually but also most of these things have no point to it you know except coolness but like driving a car at 200 for no reason just to drive fast and show everybody you can drive fast like you weren't in no emergency or even in any kind of rush to be anywhere so that is what I wanted to say like if you do something that has got a point then try to do it and it will look cool you know what I mean like the world probably hasn't even met the coolest guys because those people don't show it to anybody like the real James bond in the world you know what I mean like who has to really drive fast to escape from some situation; he won't post it anywhere so you know but obviously it's hard to live by knowing something about yourself that you know you are good at and like keeping it to yourself; the natural thing is to show everybody which is cool I guess but never ever not do something important because it doesn't look cool you know what I mean like spending time with your grandma I mean she will probably understand so that's cool but if you have a friend who is you know as everybody has made his image up and you don't hang with him in front of everybody because of that reason than that's not good you know what I mean because he won't understand that; he won't be like yeah okay because it's very unfair to except somebody to think of others before thinking about himself you know what I mean. Plus what people crave is somebody in their life who's there no matter what you know what I mean and they get that opportunity too but they let it slip away because it they spend some time in tough times for some time then the other person would feel that too and you will form an unbreakable bond of lifetime you know what I mean.

CHAPTER-6

Likes, want's And Changes

The one thing that I have noticed; I mean I do notice a lot but it is that till you have no doubt you want it; you don't get it in this world. I don't know how that law off whatever works but it is so damn true. I am sure some psychological genius must have noticed it somewhere way before even I was born but I have just come to realised that you know With everything and once you Don't have any doubts without any serious change in anything the things starts coming to you at like much faster pace on itself you know like you jump one step but now you are getting eight steps you know what I mean. Also, the things that you get but have doubts about; you are just never Fully happy in that situation anyways because obviously you can think of a situation where it's better than this. Get yourself in a situation where you are like this can't get better than this; I mean it can get better but by bringing stuff and things in this situation not by changing the situation you know what I mean. It's like that guy who is playing cool but is very scared so he's waiting for a tiny bit of unusual to happen you know what I mean like okay what was that? I am scared now; he was scared from the beginning; he was just hoping to keep it down but a little something unusual happens and it comes right out. I think with most things and people's what happens is I wouldn't say hate but disliking it or each other is the best way to liking it or each other and falling for each other because when you like straight away fall for it; your mind is just looking at this perfect painting you know what I mean but as time passes and the real stuff start coming up and you see other new paintings and so you just keep moving onto the next new painting and the next new painting because well painting are gonna keep coming. I mean sometimes you stick with and sit on a painting for some time but eventually you will start to like the new painting guaranteed but when you dislike each other at the start; you are seeing something in them that makes you change it to start liking it or person. The good thing is this is the only thing that is like set right you know what I mean like even if you like each other; you will start by acting like you dislike each other right till you can't you know what I mean whereas everything else In life is not set up right like positive thoughts and thinking's because you really have to force yourself to find positives in things and always be positive; not many people are able to do that though like turn it around which only goes to prove that with love, you can heal everything. God only bothered to set it up the right way because he knew even if everything is turned back then love is the key to turning it the right way even if you are not able to turn it the right way your entire life; it is still a pretty awesome life if you found love you know what I mean. Maybe god only made us so stupid so that we only wish for love and not get in anything serious about anything; well you know who knows, right? Which always proves my theory like even our universe is made for us to look stupid naturally until unless we go the unnatural way and not be dumb. Sometimes you know tho the person you like very much but keep acting like you dislike them when you have no doubt you want them but still you are not courageous; the universe is set up to make you courageous by making you jealous or something to give you the strength to go on; sometimes you only become stronger when the fear makes you sad not threatened you know what I mean.

We have to accept things when they are acceptable and not aim for perfection because that's quite not possible even with like our government and all other things you know because with so many people involved things will never be perfect; nobody is perfect and to add all the imperfections it just adds to you know so as long as it's acceptable don't waste your time by involving yourself in all that; I mean as a society we need to keep them in charge obviously but that cannot be our priority; we cannot be talking about that all day you know what they should do what they shouldn't basically policy making; talk about sports and talk about policy making in sports because even if somebody says something stupid; it won't anger you like that like what? How is this guy allowed to vote and in sports you get something to say to everything you know like even if your favourite team's the worst but it like stunned the no.1 team or something you know what I mean. Not just sports whatever but you can't talk about realities all day everyday because they will never take over positively; it should only be a topic of discussion if it's beyond acceptable like corruption should never be hated on I feel; movie stars act as them and earn millions and they be that all their life and not get that big pay day; I know that's not very good thinkings but still you know like if you pay a little extra; you get your delivery soon or something like that; nobody says then like whoever ordered first should get first if then it's good business then it's good business everywhere; if there corruption is leading to life and death situation for somebody else then that's not acceptable; you can steal from people but don't leave them high and dry; till there's enough for necessities and also people only talk when they don't deserve it 100%; when they deserve it 100% nobody just sits around and let it happen; even at 95% some people will let it go but when it's 100% even the weakest people like myself get up and do something about that. When you think about changing somebody the first thing that will pop in your head if you think intellectual is I need to change myself; if that's not the first step then probably you are not a bright star you know what I mean. People talk about themselves like they are giving an interview and they are not nervous at all like they already have a job so they are just giving it anyways so it's fine either way you know and the interviewer asked them so tell me what's your strengths and weaknesses? And people are giving answers like that's my weakness but actually if you think about it that's my strength you know what I mean. That's how people look at themselves and that's how we are designed to you know because for change we have to accept something but like something pops in our head and we are like we are so bad at it and then we get to know about someone who is worse at it and it just kinda makes us feel good and for some reason we feel like okay we are bad at it but there's no need for change, a few jokes from somebody worse than you and you get comfortable with sitting on whatever you should be working on and improving that. For us to feel the need to change something about ourselves a thing has to bother us repeatedly for a very long time without us getting sad from it or overcoming that sadness with like okay that's a big issue and it has costed me in the past but I can work on it without it being a issue over time and sometimes what happens is we are like okay we have been doing this and so whatever I do people will forever think of myself as that and in some cases make fun of me for that or talk to me about that or keep on embarassing me for that so what's the point of working on changing myself and get those habits out of my system and you sleep well by just sitting on it but you will never fall in love with yourselves for real like deep because what makes us love ourselves is the fight we show against the things that make us weak; most people just like to think they love themselves; they want the best for themselves and they still like themselves more than everybody don't get me wrong but deep down when they are all alone they don't fall for themselves. Even our love for ourselves don't come automatically; we have to earn, work for and deserve our love too: I guess that's why we have huge subconscious mind or something like noticing everything; we have to get ourselves out of the comfort zone and not listen to whatever's or whoever's talking in your brain asking you to chill out and rest and like get to work. Also, by making yourself comfortable; people assume in every situation like at the bar they be sitting with their friend's and having a good time and then they will see a person and they start to think like okay for a better life I have to make myself uncomfortable here; no, you don't; you don't have to make yourself uncomfortable in every situation where you are comfortable; no, you have to enjoy most moment's and that comes when you are 100% comfortable and so when you are 100% comfortable you are yourself you know and at the end of the day for a happy life you wanna go home to be with people who let you be 100% you; you don't have to work on yourself all the time; you have to enjoy yourself all the time; it doesn't come with things like you could be hanging out at paris with strangers and not be very happy but you could be in the classroom with your friends and having the time of your life even if you think you are getting bored and you need to get out of there or whatever you know what I mean. You also don't have to change things that don't look right you know most people are trying to change things that don't look right; nothing should ever be changed because they don't look right; if it don't look right but it is doing its job; it's cool; it's just your opinion vs their opinion thing and whatever you do keep it and be like I trust myself or change it like yeah many people have been calling me out on that; it's not bad to listen to people every once in a while; it doesn't matter either way like it's just a big waste of time in thinking and doing. People say stupid stuff and think it's very intellectual you know; just that emotional vibe and they say something different and they just assume it's great but it's not it's stupid like you can put thousand zeroes behind a zero and it's value would still be 0 like who out there's like okay I put 0 and it's 0; let me out one more zero and hopefully it will turn to something; oh wait it still didn't; well screw it imma keep trying; it will turn to value sooner or later you know what I mean or like people like to say if you get everything where would you put it; like we don't have space then we don't have everything in the first place now do we? And if by everything they don't literally mean everything just loads of money and property and all that then I don't think there's a person alive who's like I have too much money to buy everything like you can also buy more; donate and help people even if you keep spending it on yourself only then also there's a lot of things you could buy; nobody has had everything; this quote should never have come out; no person ever has been in a situation ever to say this thing and especially not the person who said it I can tell you that. I can go on for like a decade about all these famous quotes or whatever. I am the kind of person that I can't access a quote you know what I mean like I have to find something wrong with every quote you know what I mean and I know it's annoying or whatever but funnily enough more often than not I find something wrong with it you know what I mean but that doesn't like make me smart or something; that's not what I am saying; all I am saying is these quotes are not perfect but they are acceptable and so you can extract so much wisdom from them and grow and learn and help others also at the same time or be like me that's stupid and it doesn't make any sense; anything can be turned towards ourselves or the other side you know what I mean.

Chapter-7

Don't act on assumptions

We can't help but assume things and feel happy or sad about things or moments that's coming towards you sometimes based on our past experiences like we have been in those situations like meeting an old friend because we always have good time when we see each other or just because people told you that's it's going to be super fun or you know sometimes you are going to head into situations that are made for fun and so you assume but never act or your assumptions; go into the situation calm yourself and wait to see if your assumptions were correct like celebrities sometimes assume that particular moment will be very emotional and I would be like wow thank you for your support through the year's; I am absolutely blown away by your love and affection for me and what have you but the crowd's quite like they are not booing or nothing; they are just okay about the whole situation but the celebrity still dives into the whole emotional act based on their assumption you know what I mean like I am finding it so hard to speak right now; you guys are like super amazing and live near in my heart or something and most crowd is sitting deep in their chair; hands folded and legs streched through the next guy's chair and this guy can see the shoes off the guy behind him and so he also streched his legs long and the whole row just goes with the flow except one guy that messes it up who's not having it; so there's one guy who has legs coming under him but his cannot go anywhere you know what I mean so he's just sitting there so irritated like he just shoots the guy behind him looks like stop the process; it's not happening for me but the guy behind's not getting it so he steps on the shoes and act it's accidental and the guy behind's like ohh it's no problem and bring one leg which the guy stood on back; cleans the dirt off his shoes and streches it back again you know what I mean; so this guy who's stuck on the process like has to stretch but like the other way and not in the front to give space to the legs of the guy sitting behind you know what I mean and because of that he can't sit like leaning on the chair; he has to sit very straight you know what I mean; I mean in school they can like talk it out like hey T get your legs back or I will step or them and he actually does but in real life with strangers it's so funny to see one guy with his arms folded and legs stretched just completely frustrated looking at his family very keenly; looking and hoping to find something to get angry at them about or you know just bringing up the conversation about the fight that was all settled but you got to let the frustrations out. Anyways, the crowd like likes the celebrity but are not the crazy fans who are jumping up and down at every word; like they just finished reading a book that was very long and very boring but everybody was like that book's what literature is all about; you will learn so much and you finally finished it; you skipped some pages but you are there you know what I mean. So, now the whole moment's kinda awkward; there are two or three guys clapping like yeah wow thank you for saying you love us, man; we love you back. It's so strange in those situations like only two people clap; clapping is a group activity; it's weird if you do it alone; hoot like if you hoot alone it's still like okay makes sense; nobody hoots together even if everybody's clapping there will be one guy who will hoot and get the atmosphere going; it's made for individuals but yet; I guess people assume everyone will chime in once they start clapping and nobody does; anyways, the celebrity jumped and acted at his assumption and now it's weird and he still has to like finish his whole speech; you can't just walk off; oh okay they aren't my crowd; my bad and walk off; no, you have to complete your speech; they do try to shorten it though which keeps on making it awkwarder if that's a word like they had this whole lines on their 5-6 hard times but hoping to rush through it they just say 2 and it doesn't even seem like a struggle anymore; everybody's like that guy just got lucky and yet he thinks he got here with hard work you know what I mean. That's what we do though; we act on our assumptions like if we are meeting our favourite cousin or somebody after a long time and you just assume that it will be so energetic and so fun but when you see each other and it's strange like they are looking at you and you know they are looking at you but you keep acting like you don't know they are looking at you and you are actually looking somewhere else and then they start to look away and you get your eye's on them; it just doesn't fit right plus you can't straight jump into how life really is; at first you have to be like yeah everything's super amazing; what's with you man? After a time you can talk the truth you know what I mean; you can't just hit somebody with like man my job's getting in my head man but you know if your bond is strong everything falls in place but still never act on assumptions even when we are like we are going to have a super bad time; go in and try to communicate and talk the best off your abilities; never give anybody this impression like why am I here? I wish I was there; that would have been so fun; my life's so unlucky you know what I mean even though the other person would be like yeah dude that sounds super awesome and ask you questions like so you and your friend's do that and you start telling your stories like yeah man like my friend's are so crazy; even though they will keep standing there and act like they like hearing your stories; they don't like you and the way the life works you will find it later on like that guy's super cool and you would wanna hang out with them but they are trying to run away and give you the cold shoulder you know what I mean and it's all because of our attitude; not their fault at all; even if you hate something just get involved with a high intensity and it will turn fun like you know you know sometimes they figure that you are the most free person in the whole entire world and so they give you the responsibility of like watching after kids in your neighborhood and the kids are playing soccer you know and it just gets on your nerves when they don't understand the rules or something; you get so pissed off that you hope they get into a fight you know what I mean but you know if you walk into it with whole positive intensity and cheer as they walk into each other as tackle like yeah luke yeah show em who's the man and now the kid you cheered on gets all hyped up and he apologises to you if he makes a mistake and is like really frustrated you know what I mean; it can turn into a pretty fun time; just engaging and it can turn into a cool time but again don't engage with the purpose off showing somebody you are better than anybody even kid's; people just love to tell kids we were so much better than you when we were your age but hyping him up and treating him like a professional like sir please sit have a glass of water; after match conference for both teams together and all that stupid things can be a good time. The worst is when you are looking forward to seeing someone and you have all these thinking's in your brain like wow it's been such a long time; we will meet and have a great time catch up and everything but when you meet all you talk about is how long it's been since we were together; wow it's been that long; really, it can't be; you feel like you were having this conversation alone but now there's two people and it's not a good conversation like it's alone conversation; you don't ever want to have alone conversations in a group but it happens so often you know what I mean.

Chapter-8

No justice to looks

Nobody ever borned in the history of the world has done justice to how they look. Everybody wanna win everybody over with both looks and word's you know. We would look at how they look and look at them from far and they look so beautiful that they look so good doing talking you know what I mean; we won't hear words and we be like wow it would rock if we would get to talk to them somehow but nobody does justice to their looks; when they open their mouth; it's normal; heck most of the times it's below average; they turn out boring but we are so scared to talk to them but not scared to look at them at all and that just blows my mind; you would wait for like a few days; you would hear so many motivational videos that all you say is motivational quotes you know what I mean; you start answering to people with motivational quotes like where were you, you are late today? I ain't late; late are those people who are already gone to bed; I am 100 feet from bed and I can't wait to get more further or something; I sleep on this bed as much as the sales man of bed's who likes lays on them to show people like you will be so comfortable and it will be a good purchase or something you know what I mean. People have like started running away from you; like no I am happy with life and my efforts and so you talk to the person and they turn out to be so boring; they won't meet your information level's either and even if they do who cares? You can ask questions and learn. I wonder if like somebody was like wow I look so awesome; I have been blessed with all these; I will only answer in yes and no my entire life but that's the magic of stupid word's; nobody can resist talking even if like you are at an amazing natural site with cloud's on mountain and a little bit of sunshine but only on the Mountain top and not many people will like soak it in you know what I mean; most people will go this is amazing, right to their friend's who are with them and they will talk the whole entire time like look at that; would you look at that and that's it because people want to win over you with their words even if you already signed for a lifelong contract based on their look's and that's why everybody's on our level; nobody is above us in this world all thanks to words; it's like you know they show you this amazing house with all the facilities and carpets so soft you can sleep on them and then they say so listen the water's a problem here though; it only comes for like 2 hours and you have to wake up at 5 in the morning sometimes 3:45 to fill the water for the day or something you know what I mean like there is nobody or nothing in this World that's perfect; you can have a con for everything and so when you are feeling like okay this person is out of my league or whatever; look closely and you will find something eventually that would make you go okay that's not cool at all you know what I mean.soaking in a moment is a trait that we must try to have; that can bring peace and satisfaction in where we stand you know what I mean and it's not that hard like just find something beautiful in the place that you are at and stare at it for some time and try to think about people who are not blessed enough to have this peace and satisfaction. The longer you know a person the more you realise like they are normal; that's why I feel when like you land somebody great like let's say a great movie star start dating one of his fans; I am sure at the start of the relationship the fan would be like wow I am so lucky and you know continuosly keep saying stuff like I know how busy you are but after long time in a relationship like 3-4 years and they are not picking up their phone's or leave them hanging someplace; you won't feel like well they must be busy and I was just lucky I guess the whole time because with time you have realised we are equal; who knows maybe I am better. You realise that later but at first you are like the more people around people; the more friends somebody has and stuff like that are better people but that's not the case; that will and never was the case. Nervousness is alright; be humble but never walk away from a person on the believe that you don't deserve them and

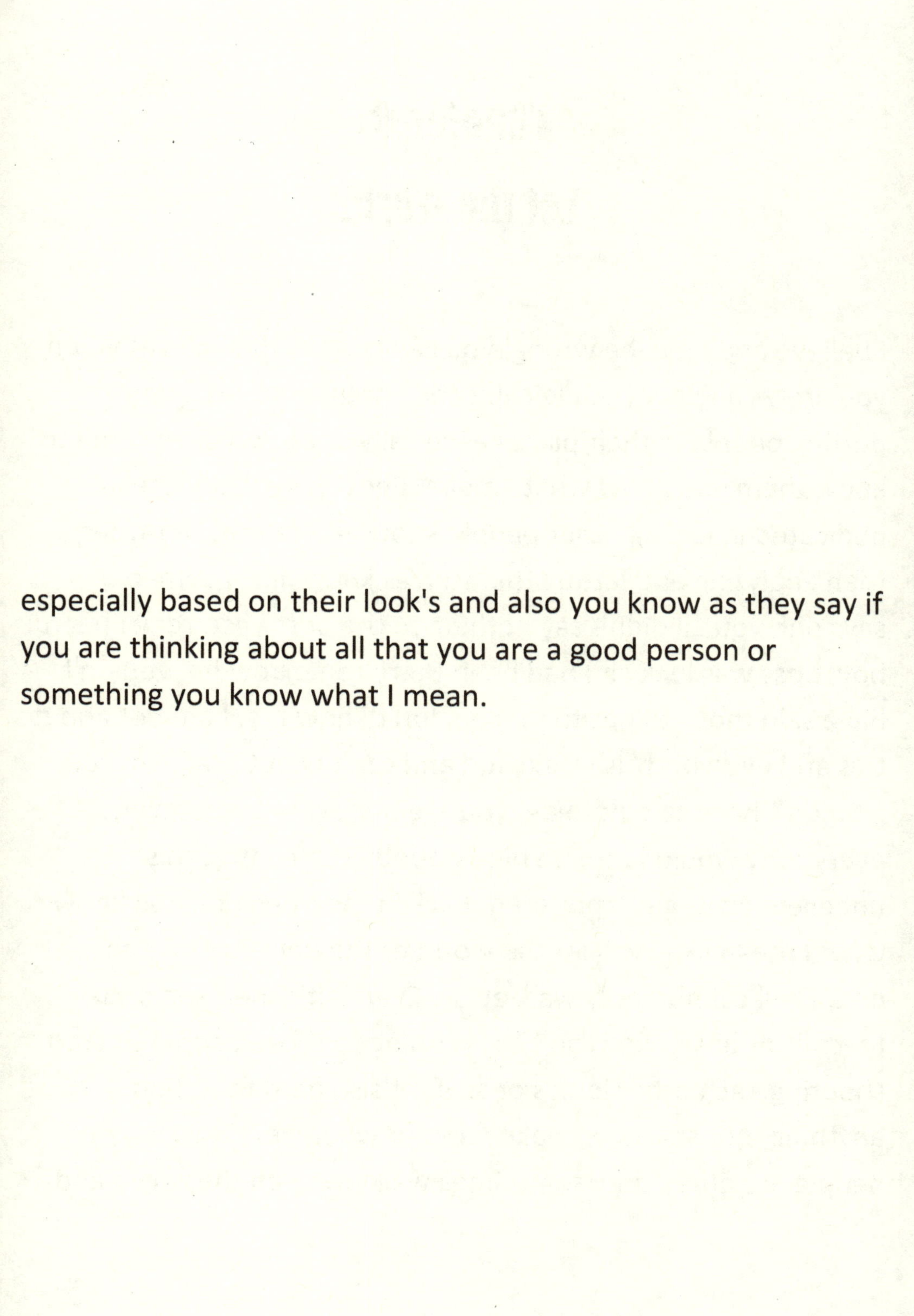

especially based on their look's and also you know as they say if you are thinking about all that you are a good person or something you know what I mean.

Chapter-9
Let the world

I believe and I maybe wrong; you can control themselves when you are wrong but people can't control themselves from putting people in their places especially once you have come to know them you know what I mean. People are like more dedicated in letting other people know where they at rather than analyzing and letting themselves know like if someone says ohh you all didn't say nothing to the boss yesterday I heard; boy, boss was lucky if I had been there tomorrow he wouldn't have said those things to me; he don't know me; I am not about this and everybody is so excited and can't wait to tell him you wouldn't have said nothing; you are one scared whatever; everybody would jump on him; nobody can control this unbelievable urge to put them back in their position you know what I mean like I will let the world or the universe take this one; I will calmly cooly walk away. Even if it's their senior like teacher or boss; they can't say nothing to those people so start shooting each other look's or scuff; it's so hard to not do anything; not smurk or make faces or whatever. Even when people are angry they sometimes walk away on their own and not engage but in this case and it's not like bad or anything but the issue is when you try to out somebody in their place and not left in on the world or the universe; they won't go away quietly; nobody will; they will come back with something to put you back in your place you know what I mean even though like yeah oh you are the one to talk about not doing anything remember that one time when you couldn't do anything you know what I mean and it gets on people's nerves even those people who knows and are at peace with what happened like yeah I can't do that; it is what it is but now since they are being targeted by someone who they wanted to you know know what he is you try to come up with excuses for that situation like yeah I only didn't do nothing in that situation because of whatever and it turns into a whole thing and it will be on your mind for hours; you will think about the whole thing when you go to bed at night. It's almost impossible to not let it get on your nerve when you try to be real with someone and they keep coming up with something and not accept what you wanted them to know about themselves and on top of them they will tell you that you are just as me or I am better than you but if you somehow is able to find the strength to let the temptation go of putting them in their place and let them talk to you about how big they are even though it will be in your head like how the hell does he think so much about themselves when they are so stupid but you won't be like angry and you know finding someone to talk about it and somebody agreeing with you over him just cools you down like yeah man you are exactly right; how does he; remember few days ago when he said that. Sometimes when you find people to agree with you over people it can be years and the situation won't change but you are alright with it like that's just life like all the same people are in your life as it is and nothing's changed and you and the dude still talk about how can he be so fake all the times you know what I mean. Also, what you need to realise is people don't change over what somebody says to them; it's the teachings of life and universe that can humble you you know what I mean; I mean it can shake them for a couple of days if it's something really deep but they will be back to where they was like chewingum in your pocket; it can get a little doozy but you know it's still chewable; it's always chewable. Also, the thing we don't realise is we are actually jealous of them like they are in the same position as you in their life but they still at least at the top feel and are so hyped up about themselves whereas you just feel so bad like why are things not falling in place for me; why is this happening to me? Their perspective on life can be whatever but at the end of the day they solved the puzzle on how to be happy and if it's always this that they could have done that if that or if they were or whatever then so be it; at the end of the day we are all chasing happiness and finding reasons to be happy and if being like that makes you happy then I guess we need to be more like them like always thinking our place is way better than so be it and also you know maybe we are the one's that are the fake one's like we always think we are better but what if we are not better; we are worse than them; we are one's judging other people you know what I mean so you know somehow keeping your lip shut and let the universe take care off it if it needs to be taken care of and I am not a psychiatrist or anything but what if they feel so bad deep down that they need to be like that to not drive themselves crazy like believing their lies and not accepting that they couldn't have done anything in that situation; I am not brave enough to do anything about that so they just believe their lies that because of that they couldn't. I mean when those people say yeah I know I was right there but I decided to not say anything because I was like whatever but you know me I didn't want to make it a big deal because I am already on their bad list because of what I said that time; you wouldn't know anything about it; you are soft you are not tough like me. When they say that it's so hard to be just like yes sir oaky dokey and walk off but the thing to remember is they also know what happened in there and how they was feeling so if they are not able to like understand that; you won't be able to make them understand that so you know keep that mindset of it is what it is and a whole lot of confrontation and negative thinking will stop if you ask me. If anything start joking around like yeah man he doesn't know what you are about; make them your friend but also don't like just keep sitting there joking for hours; there should always be that just a guy I see everyday; we don't talk much vibe you know what I mean because if you get over friendly they will start hanging out with you more and more and that's not cool. At the very least if they are already in your friend circle and hang around with the same people as yours and so you can't go anywhere; keep it awkward when you two are alone; never let it be comfortable to say whatever when you are alone you know what I mean because you will never have fun because once you find this characteristic in somebody it's hard for you to have a good time with them you know what I mean so always just reply with okay with faces like what you talking about and hope for long pauses in conversation; make them overly explain their point and still act like you don't get whatever they are talking about or whatever you know what I mean.

Chapter-10

The reason

We have all heard like everything's happening for us not to us and that there's a reason for everything that's going on right now for us to take our lessons but I believe taking lessons happens automatically; we don't have to do nothing for that; when you do it enough times you will just be experienced enough to realise like that's not right and I shouldn't do that that's why the older you get the mature you become; that's not a fact but you know what I mean. The way I see it like it will start to pile on you and you will be tested and then one day you will get your reasons for all that's happened or maybe you will not but you will for sure be free from it over a period of time and then something else will start to pile on you; it's basically like waste in your dustbin like it will pile on and then sooner or later you will throw it out and it will start to fill up again; that's why they say happiness is in chasing goals not acheiving goals because you will spend more time on the workings and all that and a very less time with the feeling of winner I guess because even as a winner you won't stop getting tested; you will have to face some kind of battle everyday and it's hard to celebrate the night before and then face your opponents; nobody's free from that; you can reach any stars in this world and you won't ever stop getting tested you know what I mean and that's exactly why I feel it's stupid like to think like I want to be a millionaire and then all my problems will be gone; yeah these problems will be gone but there would be another problems and more often than not bigger problems than you are facing right now so only happy to be happy I guess is finding little positives; negativity around is much bigger than positivity like dropping your gold earrings in sewer line or something and you will have to dig hard but the rewards the god damn gold earrings. When things get tough though and you feel like your hand can't reach for that gold earring and you just want to get out of here; get clean and eat something; then at this point you will have to change your perspective; you can't keep the same perspectives you started with whatever your started with; when you keep thinking of reason for acheivement of that goal like if I get that gold earrings I will buy myself a car and not have to go to work in this train or whatever; one of these days when it will get easy and the train ride is not that bad; you would be like you know what this isn't that bad and maybe I should just take train rides

I guess and that's when you have to change your perspective because you have to keep going after that car and so find something else whatever that might be because our brain thinks everything; that's his job and for everything even if it's pretty sure about something and it is giving you hundreds of thinking's and thoughts for doing that; it will slip in one or two negatives one's too over time like if it's good and that's what you want it will start with positive ones but if you keep thinking about it day and night eventually it will send you a little bit of negative energy to calm you down or something I guess so we have to give it different reasons for acheiving it for it to have no doubts. What people do is that if something goes right and something goes wrong then they will put all their energy in fixing the things that went wrong but like the first step should always be in making sure the things that went right stay that way; that those things also don't start to go wrong and that's just plain wrong especially if you are drifting apart and not spending as much time with your family, never assume everything will be alright because people react to your energies and give you back the same energy; it's plain simple; the level you show somebody that you are willing to put them on in your life is also the same level they are going to put you on; even though they are your family and they are supposed to love you unconditionally but still you have to give something everytime to receive something; you can't expect it to always be like that without you doing anything and being like past; that's just straight facts and that is why most couple's over a while start to ask themselves what happened to us? When and how did we become like this? It been quite a well too; it starts with a little crack like you ignoring them on something or not acting like before like if they told you I got a cut and you are like ah it's not a big deal; it will heal itself or something. The other person would be like yeah I know it's just I wanted you to like whatever and then this will stay in their mind's and then small crack will start to become bigger and even if you been going non-stop to give them a better life and fulfill their dream's; you have lost them and it really sucks when you get and acheive the dream you had or the goals you had but the reason you were doing it for no more seems relevant or close to you or something you know what I mean; even in success it feels like boy I wasted a lot of my time chasing a bunch of nothing; why did I work so hard I can't remember.

For people who are like I still don't know my purpose or what I was born to be; first and foremost there's no age at which it comes; you maybe 35 and one day you see something and it fascinates you so much that you are like I want to do that and you will get to it and don't worry it won't be like you be 45 and you will find your purpose to be a soccer player; it does not work like that; you will find something that's acheivable but like it's very hard and you will go okay I can do this; that is why you will find it so fascinating in the first place. The other thing is that there's no guarantees Everybody's purpose would not be to change the world or something; it can be small but it will matter and it will affect us for better. It's like you have all these hard drives and all that artificial intelligence stuff that has like information of everybody from all across the world and you could be the toilet in the A.I room and if you weren't there then one of these days somebody would have been like in rush or something to go to the bathroom which is upstairs and forget to close the chamber or something correctly and lots of data gets leaked you know what I mean like I have no problem being a toilet you know what I mean like in sports what some players do does not show up on the stat sheet but they placed a huge role in getting that win.

CHAPTER-11

Who's loss?

You need to ask yourself what is it that I am great at? What sets me apart? And if the answer in your head not on your mouth is absolutely nothing then you are great at thinking humbly which is not that easy; it's quite unique actually because our brain would send something to like make us feel okay like to cover your sadness sooner or later it will send you something to make you feel great but like if the answer is straight no then because of your thinking humbly everybody is like lucky and blessed to have you around and if they don't want you around they are actually pretty stupid and it's their loss; you are okay you need to think about or find something voluntarily to be great at. I mean think about it how many people you know that think humbly and if you know somebody like that how great are they to hangout with; they never ever make you feel bad about anything so if you are that person; who's loss is it; theirs or yours? I would bet everything I have on theirs which is not much like I don't have much so I won't win huge but I will win.

The thing is you should think serious but say funny but people are thinking funny or thinking scary because that's what they think they need to think to be funny which is not true; I mean maybe for a standup comedian but then he's seriously thinking about something funny so I guess I am right, right? So you know my point being most people don't know how to think; they just start to think about something that they saw or whatever conversation they are having or were having like hey did you notice how stupid Jake was behaving at the party or whatever and then they would get to the thinking but they won't by themselves make time and think about everything and how and why people were behaving like that and that's how you get answers to who is important and who's not because when you are thinking because somebody started that topic then your thinking is going to be affected a little by them even though you will have your own thoughts or whatever and you will still keep seeing people the way you are seeing if you know them; if you don't know them then they can probably plant something in your head but you are making time to think by yourself that's when there are no topics; you are going to be thinking about what's really important and what really matters and that's when you find out that okay that person and I are definitely not like before but why is that? I mean they are simply amazing; are they being like that because I am not paying them that attention or something?

Another great thing about thinking is try to not think about the thought's that are popping in your head but think about the reason why they are popping in your head; most people just roll with the thought's like I see candy; candy is cool; we shouldn't eat many of those too because they are not healthy or whatever and so you would think this is a positive conversation that you are having with yourself or positive thinking basically and that wow I am so smart but you will never think about something you don't know; deep down you already knew that so it was just a waste of time so when you think about the reason that these are popping in your hear you will be like there's absolutely no reason for me to think about damn candy right now; candy was just passing by; I need to forget that. Another thing about thinking humbly and why you are special is that most people when they think of something great about themselves they would just make something up and think they are the only one who would do that but it's everybody who would do that or should do that you know what I mean; thinking about something you are great at which everybody is great at is still better than thinking about being fake great you know what I mean like being scared but thinking I am brave and living on the excuses about why you were not brave in that situation last time but you will be very brave the next time or how you weren't brave because nobody else was doing anything so you was all alone and that's just stupid for me to do something there; people need to be beaver for me to be braver and so basically it's not my fault you know what I mean so basically what I am trying to say is they are lucky to have you around and they for their whole life will wish for or talk like we never met somebody like that their entire life I can guarantee you that.

Also,you are great at something; some days you have bad days and just the thing you wanted to be great at didn't go as well but like that was just a bad day you know; you are not like that everyday or you won't be like that everyday; all you need to do is not compare yourself with anybody and have a mind which you have that knows what you need to work on all the time like let's say you were a basketball player and you are shooting on one net and your family's watching and on the other net another kids shooting and he is sinking his shoots one after one and you are missing every time and so you would wanna get out off that court as soon as possible and every past shot would be on your mind taking that new shot and you would go home and be like I have been working so hard; being so disciplined and everything and still I am not at that kids level; after giving so much I am still not at his level; i will never be at his level so what's the point but who knows it was his best day on the court or your worst? Getting up is not easy and that example I gave was a sports one where everything's visible like okay he's technically great, he's not rushing or taking bad shots; he's just missing the shots; that's okay he's just having a bad day but in other aspects where you can't see the margins that clearly; you are like okay maybe I am not good enough and other's would be like that too like man you are not good enough straight up; I am just being honest man you know what I mean so you know keep going because people won't start recognising you till you make it very obvious for them; think from your perspective would you see what's inside other people; no, you won't; you probably won't be as hard on them if you are a good person like but still you can't see what they are made of; that's something only they can see and so make it clear and obvious and that you can only do but picking yourself up every god damn time and being your biggest supporter and the worst critic and you know it's not that hard; we do it with everything anyways; we all have that white and red guys on our shoulder like as they show us in movies like you know what I mean. Also, we have this weird habit where we think what if we work hard and not get better like that's probably the dumbest thought ever; if you are sitting in a car. You know what that is such a dumb thought; I am not even going to give an example or address that at all just go on and work on your craft as much as you can.

Chapter-12

Care and choosing people

The first thing we need to remember when choosing person for us is that you can't change them; I mean probably the goodness of your heart can but don't work with that believe because people see movies and the hero's like I have been moving from person to person but there's something about you that makes me stop and be yours forever; now you might be that good to turn them but never think that because you might set yourself up for a heartbreak you know what I mean. think most of the people often choose the most fun person to be around most of the time; not the most beautiful; some people like even start hating beautiful people after an age but everybody wants to be around a fun guy and that can like affect any relationship no; I mean I believe I am not married or in a relationship of any sorts but people who are if they have been in a relationship for long must be open with like wow they are beautiful and the other person's like yeah you are not wrong but fun; ohh he's so funny and then I don't think you can stay cool like yeah yeah he is; I don't think so. Anyways, there comes a time when you have to choose what you need; a fun relationship or responsible relationship. Now, if you decide to roll with the fun one then you will have to put in some work and take some responsibilities like you know what I mean but people want people who are fun and responsible and hope both quality can co-exist but one side is definitely more than the other in every person you know and it can change also like the person who gets stressed out big time over small things will have lower total stress in his life over a person who don't worry about thing's as much you know what I mean because he will always look to do it perfectly and leave nothing behind because well he will get stressed at the time off leaving like if I leave it alone then ohh no no that can happen and ohh god that can happen too but a person who's like what's the big deal; it's cool let's go out and enjoy; we will get it done in the morning will be under great amount of stress in the morning like oh get up run eat whatever just run you know what I mean. That's my point like the person who takes stress easily is the not fun one but he will get it done like everything would be done for you even like 20 years down the line like all kinds of policies or whatever for whatever happens we are prepared kind of a thing and so you will be prepared. Now, is this the type of person you should get together with? But imagine like okay we will not be prepared for most things if we go with the fun one but what if we don't face much in the time ahead you know what I mean like we will figure it out maybe not as better then the other relationship I could have been in but it will be alright and everything would be fine. So, what should we do? This is my opinion only which maybe right or wrong I don't know but I believe you should choose either way and if they love you they will change in whatever direction you want them to turn into; things rub off on each other if you spend time together; not totally but there's always change you know what I mean like all of a sudden you both won't be taking too much stress or not stress at all but if something stresses you out big time and your partner knows that and it doesn't stress him out at all then also he would get it done because they are in love with you. Relationship's like that 3-5 pm dull time when there is half sun and half shadow you know what I mean like it's a different vibe; nobody is planning to do anything in that time like everybody is planning for something later or thinking about earlier but that time everybody just wants passed; that time just has that kind of a energy especially if you like don't take naps or is at office at that point of time; that time does not go well but as soon as that half sun goes away it's moving energy like we are not getting bored let's do something you know what I mean.

Then sometimes people are like well at least I have your memories or whatever and the thing about memories is good memories make you sad because they are not happening right now and bad memories make you angry like why I did this; why I acted like that. There are no memories in relationship; memories are huge in friendships and all other relationships you know what I mean like even if your friend isn't there or like you haven't met in a real long time you can still like tell people about it and be very happy you know what I mean like it can lead to further activities with your new friends like man, one time me and this friend of mine did this and oh my god it was the best time ever and your new friend would probably be like oh that's great bro; let's do it or maybe bro that's nothing me and my friend used to do this you know what I mean; it's stupid tho how like when you tell somebody this is what me and my friend did they appreciate it for a minute and then back it up with a great fun story off their own; nobody wants anybody to have had more fun than them in the past like but in future they are jealous like ohh you are going to Dubai next week; wow, you are so lucky; then nobody says ohh you are just going to Dubai; I am planning on going to Amsterdam bro you know what I mean so my point being memories are not good; good or bad they ain't good; they just hold us from having a great good time now.

Chapter-13

Speakings

I mean I don't really like think about things; I just throw them out there out of my guts or like things that pop in my head but I don't really think because thinkings is very confusing to some of us like there's always pro and con with everything and then I am not someone who looks at it like reasonably like okay this thing has more pro than con so let's do it or this has more con than pro let's not do it; I am always like okay yeah that's great but still you know what I mean like even if something has twenty good things and three bad things I am going to do it half heartedly and that is if I choose to do it so I don't really like to think about things was my point so keeping that in mind what I wanted to say was this like when you are standing still like not in motion and you are speaking; you are speaking to impress you know what I mean like if you are moving then maybe you are not speaking to impress like bye I have to go; I catch up with you later or like if you ask somebody where's the 8th Street or something but when you are standing still you are definitely speaking to impress and that even goes for all the world leader's and all the great people like even if In their actions they helped many people even if they had to sacrifice something off their own but in speakings everybody wants to impress you know what I mean even if they are like saying that don't try to impress anybody or let anything stop you from doing this they are hoping you are like wow he's great you know what I mean. In motion though you maybe not thinking's of impressing somebody then maybe you are just hoping that it stays neutral you know what I mean like hopefully they don't take it in a negative way and hopefully what we said when we was moving Doesn't affect the things we said when we were sitting like so my point being you shouldn't really be angry to yourself over what you said or why you want people to be so damn impressed with everything you said because that's the most normal thing in the world if our gurus and all these great people who have no wish for anything in this life and have sacrificed everything of theirs can't help but hoping for people to be impressed by what they say; how can you and I? you know what I mean. Even people who only move forward like I don't care what anybody things off me or what they say about me; those people also want people to be like what they hear when they says I don't care about your opinions on myself; I am going to continue being myself. You can control speaking that make people angry like that's in your hand; you know what you are doing when you are saying hurtful things and you can control that no matter how hard you find controlling yourself but you can't control like saying something that makes things awkward or saying something and people breaking it down in a completely different way than what you had hoped for you know what I mean. All we have is our actions and that's what we need to control. A great exercise I feel for that is to like play team sports and being happy when your team has the ball even if you haven't touched it for a minute or two like some player's aren't really happy even if there team has it; they want it in their hands or at their feet and then they are nervous like what do I do with it because it's a responsibility to not to commit a turnover or a mistake; to be genuinely happy for your teammates and celebrating their success goes a long way I am telling you and it can be done like even if you feel like you aren't that type of a person who feels happy like that even for your own people; it's just natural you can't help it. No, you are wrong; it can be done. Let me tell you how; start to clap and fake laughing and giggling when they suceed no matter how bad you don't want to and then they will fake it too when you suceed and then it will become a tradition kind of a thing and before you know it you will be having fun in your team's success genuinely you know what I mean like you keep faking something for so long; it turns more real than real you know; we move away if we find something or somebody fake but actually there's a huge opportunity there. sometimes . It's just settings things In motion and before you know it you are doing the right things and you are happy with yourself that you are doing the right thing; the world thing is just the energy thing like people don't realise energies work like people be wondering why x not be treating me like before and not as happy to see me like before because your energy is like okay I want to talk to the other person like you know what I mean; it's very rare for you to have be focused on somebody deeply and them for not to be on the same level; I am not talking about love relationship's here because your energies aren't equal in that case you know what I mean like you are in love with somebody from the first time you saw and maybe they didn't fall for you so that's a different thing but once you are in a relationship and your energy is fully towards them; they will respond you know what I mean like some people are like I am doing all the right things and buying gifts and everything but we are not like before; it's because of the energy, mate like yes, you are buying gifts but you are not excited to buy those gifts or yes you are making dinner but you are not really happy to be making dinner for them; you are just making it because you feel like you should or like let's say you bring pizza over but you take your slice and go and watch TV; energy is everything you know what I mean even if like you don't do the stuff but you have dedicated positive energy; it works like let's say you go home and you didn't get the gift but you genuinely forgot and you wish you had and your energy shows that; it won't like affect anything; like if your energy genuinely says that you are sad you can't afford all the great things for your family; I don't think they will be like I don't know whatever just get me that you know what I mean or they aren't really family you know what I mean. That is why even when you bother somebody; you get closer than ever because your energy is like I care for you tho. Another thing that team sport's teaches us is like we aren't really happy with the winners winning like everybody wants the underdog to win and parents need to address that like who are you cheering for? Oh I am hoping for this team to win. Why son? Because I don't want them to win. You have to address that like that's not a good thing to hope for the best team to lose; it's affecting your character like if they are the best you should be happy for them and clap for them you know what I mean.

I don't think we should give people that positive thinking stuff because that just doesn't make sense at all like when you think positive you will believe and everything like yeah that's what positive thinking is; it's like you have to stay in hotel no. 202 then you stay inside the room right; you don't go in front of it like that's what it is like they are like think positive because it will make you believe in your goals but like we can acheive our goals is thinking positive; that is the first step; people are like so how do we think positivitely so that we can believe we can acheive what we want to acheive; there's no thinking positively; that's keeping positive mindset which comes from thinking positively which is step-2: first step is yes I can do it which is thinking positively which comes and goes and when it stops going that's when you have positive mindset; even if it like keeps coming and going for all your life; that's not a problem either; you can still acheive all kinds of success in your life you know what I mean like you may not be number-1 but you can make it to the top and it comes from work too sometimes likes okay I have put in so much work but sometimes it may not come no matter how much time you put in but just participate no matter how hard your hearts pumping like once you participate you will realise like wow they are not better than me; I can win this. You will not be as calm and will commit mistakes when you don't have that confidence before the start but once you do and that's why they probably say like it doesn't matter how you start; it only matters how you end it you know what I mean.

Chapter-14
Unlocking people

I think everybody expect the other person to react in a particular way like if I do this they should do that; if I do that then they should do that you know what I mean. Like they say in movies every person has a price and people really believe that and when they find out that they are not reacting to it in the way they thought which in their mind is the only way that you were supposed to react to that in that situation; they get angry because they have no answers then you know what I mean like you are going somewhere okay and you hadn't reached where you wanted but your gps is telling you to go where you are going and you find out you were going the wrong way from the start like you have to turn back 5 hours to get on the right road; your house from where you started is like half an hour away but where you want to go is like still far far away and the person is obviously so angry and instead of going home and calling it a day it's ego thing now like no I am making something of today; I will reach there like I am not calling them to say I ain't coming today; they would think I am a liar you know what I mean and this is the big issue especially in love side of things where it's all on the line like people fall for somebody and they are like it will be everything if we get that person and if we do this and do that I expect them to behave in this way like everybody even if they are like I don't know how to talk and I get nervous or whatever they still believe like if I do this or say this they will be here one day and once you find out that that person does not react to it the same way like it didn't work on them at all; you are angry because well you wasted a lot of time and people shouldn't expect anything; it should always be somewhere in your mind that everything I do may not matter at the end like all that I do may not unlock this person to me at all so let's roll you know what I mean like always be prepared to be wrong and people are in other things; they have doubts even if they are working hard day and night on other things but in love if the other person is reacting positively; they are like they will for sure get unlocked you know what I mean. Plus, every person like thinks so different than one another like I meet so many people everyday whose imagination and like other things are so beyond me you know not everybody has everything but this guy is superior than you in this and way behind in something else and that guy is superior to you in that and way behind in something else you know what I mean like in school time there was this girl and she was my art and craft class partner and so teacher would ask us to draw something on a white paper and everytime it was like me and her brain would go on a walk to figure out what to draw on that page and there would come a big wall and I would stop there while she would jump over that and god knows where she would go and then come back and meet me in a matter of seconds you know what I mean like she would always have this amazing imagination which I could never ever get close to and so for me to think doing all these and these would make her like me or look she's laughing at my jokes or whatever would make her like me would be wrong; I mean maybe they would; I didn't actually try to be really honest; I wanted to but I didn't; anyways, that is my whole point like you can't imagine it would work. Even if what you have done has worked on past 1000; don't mean it will work on 1001; always be set up for failure and if you get angry or frustrated take it out on them at least because it was your thoughts and thinking's that told you the edge is 1 km away; the sea didn't say nothing so keep swimming till it comes I guess.

Chapter-15

How to help doesn't come automatic

There are three types of people in this world. Good; not so good and bad. I am not sure about it like at all but it's not a bad assumption to assume like there's 5% good and 5% bad people. Good people suffer the most; not so good don't suffer so much; they don't get in any trouble where they already know they can't win you know what I mean like even if you are like Billy gets into fights all the time; yeah, because he believes he will win and it's not for any good; now is it? Bad people may suffer a lot or may not suffer a lot; it all depends on their mindset, the situations and reasons for them becoming a bad person. Now most people don't actually meet not one good or bad people in their whole entire life. Isn't that amazing; you don't meet good or bad people your whole entire life. Even if you do meet the bad it would be for a very small period of time; I mean that small period can change your life for ever but still it won't be for long because well you will go to any measure to avoid those people. In any case you can't avoid those people if they decide to come around you know what I mean; you can't help it really so you know worry definitely worry but don't stress it you know what I mean like always be on your toes; always be calm; always be nice to everybody even on bad day's because in this world you read the god damn newspaper for a day or listen to news on t.v and you will realise smallest of smallest things can trigger anybody; even if they are not bad people; the not good people when they think they can take you on; they want to take you on to prove to everybody else what they think of themselves. The funny thing is all the good things you know about yourself; if they are true you won't need nobody's stamps but if they are not you will automatically bring them up and hope people agree you know what I mean like somewhere deep down like your subconscious mind knows somehow; I don't really know how it works but it works for sure. Like somewhere deep down you know what you are really about but it's very hard to accept I guess that I am not strong at all or whatever you know what I mean like it makes you very sad that you won't be able to do anything but the thing is everybody is there and yes it is very hard to accept yourself but the thing is we all have enough to be anything in this life like if you are hoping that you would be like this cool spy guy that they show in movies and you will run through the entire city and they will shot you 200 times and it won't connect and you shoot 1 time and get all of them then that's actually not going to happen; it's not impossible but I believe 1 in 1000000 would actually have that kind of a day you know. Nothing is impossible except for everybody doing the impossible; that's set for a special bunch of people who for damn sure have accepted themselves for who they are but the thing is with society we can be that strong you know what I mean. We just have to teach ourselves how to help? People think that comes automatically but it doesn't; it needs to be taught. It's the dumbest thing about all the schools around the world to accept people will learn how to help on their own like to assume if we give them good education; they will help people; that's like asking an athelete who can run all day to play soccer or a specific sports you know what I mean like they can run faster than anybody on the pitch but playing a sports is more than athleticism; you need a special set of skills too. The first thing that should be taught after a,b,c,d stuff is how to help and it should be a subject that should go all the way from like nursery to your college education. That's the only hope right now that we have off having a better world to teach everybody how to help; maybe there's; I am not sure but for me this should start ASAP you know what I mean; every generation is getting more and more greeder and mean and so many people who need help Don't get help even if people want to help; they have no idea how to no matter the level of education they have. We need to teach people to stand up if you see something wrong; this should be like our code on earth like you always stand with the truth no matter how scary it is and when we start doing that; there are more good people than bad people and even bad people won't turn to bad when they will have help you know what I mean like if all the rich people made this rule like for rich community like the highest salary we can have is 1 crore per month like that is sufficient for us to live a good life till there's like hunger on this planet like once there is no hunger or nothing; then we go on and be as rich as we want to be but first we need to make sure nobody dies of hunger when we have so god damn much you know what I mean.

Like even our elder's; we don't even know how to help our parents; I for damn sure don't know. There's that whole thing like they went through the same thing as us at our age is like not true at all; the whole world's different know; they also went through same sort of stuff like us you know what I mean but like there's a whole lot of difference between driving a car that goes 40 and driving a car that goes to 300 you know what I mean like you can say I know how to drive a car but you can't really tell the dude at 300 what to do no matter how much you want to. The whole thing for them is so strange like we would be laughing and having a great time and then we will excuse ourselves to go to the bathroom for a minute and we will check our phones in the bathroom and see something that we don't like and we would come out of the bathroom in a completely different mood you know what I mean like they are like what happened? You was just laughing and we don't really know how to answer those questions because the answers are so petty like we are ourselves wondering why is it making me sad; why do I care so much about something that doesn't even affect me in any ways you know what I mean. We imagine our parents would be like okay because they went through the same sort of thing when they were our age but they didn't really you know what I mean. They are so confused and rightly so and we ourselves are confused too like there is a way you live which is ignore what's going on your head but then there's all these things on social media or whatever like speak your mind and be real or whatever and now you are half here half there you know what I mean like imagine a world where everybody said everything they thought or said like it is so hard to think good about somebody all the time like for no reason what so ever you don't like nobody else's driving even if you are a horrible driver because there's a reason and you know that but you don't have their reason and why they are driving like that you know what I mean like without reason everything's negative in your head. Why are they wearing this? Why is they showing off? Why would they do that? Once you have the reason you are like okay makes sense. Reasons turn negativity into positivity. That's why I believe that whole thing like you don't have to explain anything to your friends or your enemies because your friends will understand anyways and enemies will not understand no matter what. I believe you have to explain; if anything in this world if you stay quiet on; you are guilty you know what I mean like in the perfect world you shouldn't have to explain anything but our world is exactly opposite off the perfect world and all these quotes are made for the perfect world and so they sound good but they won't work. Just talk to the oldest friends of yours; the closest one like you have been close for past 20 years and listen to what you guys are talking about; either you are talking about the third person or something else but if you are talking about each other to each other; you are just giving each other reasons for what you did you know what I mean like for everything like hey man saw your snap; you went to that cafe. Yeah man, my mother asked me to pick it up from there and blah blah blah. Without reasons there is no conversation; without giving reasons every single day no two friends can even have a conversation. Even with your parents like they will love you no matter what but still they need reasons for everything. Just notice the amount off reasons conversation we have; almost all off them you know what I mean. Nobody can not give reasons; I mean I don't know how the dude who gave this quote lived without giving any reasons; maybe he didn't even know he was giving reasons like you give reasons for good things also you know what I mean like let's say you bring your wife cake; she would be like wow but what's the occasion; husband would be like ohh I just thought it would be lovely to have a long talk and some cake or whatever but like he's giving a reason for the good he did. If people don't ask you still give reasons like wow sir what a lovely song; yeah, I just thought people are so sad these day's so why not I cheer them up you know what I mean like you give reasons in good, bad and when nobody's even asking. So many people are Begging their loved ones to please just give me a chance to explain you know what I mean and they don't even have a reason; they were just being plain stupid so. In jobs and business; let's just say spend one day without giving any reason for your actions and see what happens. People are stupid anyways; everybody knows there is no perfection in this world like there is scope for everything to get better you know what I mean and everybody knows that yet everybody is chasing perfection and it is not going to happen everybody knows that but still and that leads to unhealthy things like so many people are like you do one bad thing and people forget all the good you have done and that's true if anything people instead of remembering the good things they imagine even worse things that you might have done you know what I mean like if you fail an exam even your parents are like he's definitely doing something bad we don't know about; maybe he's smoking cigarettes or something you know what I mean like you will be judged for everything; just look at sports like everybody knows every now and then you will have a bad game; it just happens no matter if you were perfect before that game like with sleep and diet or whatever but still it happens and yet people will pass judgement. That's why you shouldn't even commit one mistake because then it would be like he must be capable of doing more like maybe this is just the start; one mistake and you won't ever be trusted like before; I mean even if you stop after doing something bad; it will take some huge time to repair everything. We have to understand bad spreads like fire and good might not spread at all; even if it is lucky enough to spread; even then thought of bad will take over.

What to do?

I think I can be wrong but this is my belief that things don't stop affecting us as we grow older like let's say cigarettes; you can say to a kid smoke them when you grow older but they will still be bad for health no matter what you know what I mean; we have a better understanding off what it does to us; you don't know that when you are a kid but it still affects us in a bad way; same goes for movies. I would suggest to watch comedy movies and sitcoms that they say are funny but aren't really but still watch them because they can have a positive impact on you; like you see the main guy always being light in situations and that can rub off on you but people keep watching action movies you know single guy taking over or old historical dramas or whatever and they won't teach you anything; I mean there's a lesson to take from all anything but that is when you are really looking for it and even when you are looking for it; there's no guarantees you will take the right lesson out of it you know what I mean but those funny serial and family sitcoms can rub off on you and make us be more calm and happy.

Also, do justice to the talents god has blessed you with; everyone's like be happy with being different as a person and people are now actually happy with being different; I mean not all but there are some people who have accepted that and even people who are different and unique but people are telling them to be like them; they can't turn no matter what; they might turn themselves off but they won't turn into normal and stop being different; people keep searching for people who accept them for who they are so that's fine but in your craft and business and all that; people are not happy with being different and unique; unique things take time for people to understand them you know; now they are more salesman than craftsman and that's not doing justice to the talents god blessed you with. I mean obviously you need stuff to sell to make money but turn into a salesman not be a salesman you know what I mean like if the thinking and thoughts going into it is let's figure out what people like; what they want to see. That's not doing justice to god's blessing which is your talent. Make it genius and then turn into a salesman; people can go lick an ostrich during the creating process. What you are doing should make people's life better not bad; that shouldn't change but what it is should be completely unique and reflect you as a person or a company and that is what's going to take you all the way and make you a brand; if you turn into a salesman before everything; you may start earning good profits pretty early as compared to the other way but that will only go to a point. Plus if what you are offering is unique and fresh then even if they don't like you; they can't help coming to you. We are humans;

this is our biggest gift; if we were animals there's a fixed king and there are fixed roles and fixed positions for you that you get the day you were born; you can't change that but we as humans can; nobody knows who's going to end at the top; it is dependent on the time we put into our craft; how patient we are with whatever time it takes people to understand our uniqueness and where we are coming from and a bit of luck I guess too but luck I believe favors everybody at some point of time; nobody has gone through their entire life being unlucky at every road; they might think they have but that cannot be the case.

In the end if they don't understand your uniquesness then don't be sad; it's their loss. Don't think I am stupid; no, you are smart because you can figure them out but they can't figure you out; you have something new to offer; they absolutely don't; they might tweak it a little and think it's new but it's not; even people who are like way above you with where they are in their career might not be unique; they might also be walking on the same road so don't worry about anybody and keep being unique.